I Love You,
Winnie the Pooh

Ellen Titlebaum
ILLUSTRATED BY Robbin Cuddy

Disney
PRESS

New York

FIRST EDITION
1 3 5 7 9 10 8 6 4 2
Library of Congress Card Number: 98-89404
ISBN: 0-7868-3227-4
For more Disney Press fun, visit www.DisneyBooks.com

I Love You,
Winnie the Pooh

The sun was setting in its favorite spot behind the elm trees in the
Hundred-Acre Wood. Winnie the Pooh was seated on the very best
log for seeing the sunset. And his very best friend, Christopher
Robin, was right beside him.

"What a wonderful day this was, Pooh," said Christopher Robin.
"We hunted for heffalumps, chased butterflies, and—"

"Ate lots and lots of honey sandwiches!" added Pooh cheerfully.

Christopher Robin laughed and gave the stout little bear a big hug. "I love you, Pooh. You're the Best Bear in the World!"

Pooh suddenly felt very happy—even happier than when he'd
just eaten a pot of warm honey. The two friends said good-bye, and
with a bounce in his plump step, Pooh set off for home.

Later that evening, Pooh snuggled down in his cozy bed and pulled the covers up to his chin. Soon he was dreaming about being the Best Bear in the World.

A bear as smart as Christopher Robin. As neat as Piglet. As bouncy as Tigger. And since he was as organized as Rabbit, the Best Bear always had a full honeypot nearby. Or possibly two full honeypots.

And so it was that a grumble in his tummy woke Pooh from his happy dream.

Morning sun spilled through his window, warm and golden, as Pooh yawned and stretched. "Dum-de-dum," he hummed. "Now that I'm a Best Bear, I'll do Best Bear things everywhere."

But Pooh did not know quite what a Best Bear would do first.
Pooh thought and thought. "The best thing to do in the morning is
have breakfast," he said finally. "So that's what a Best Bear would
do!" He started off for Rabbit's house.

Rabbit was surveying his garden. "The cabbage heads are ahead of schedule. And these carrot tops are just the tops," he chuckled.

"Hello, Rabbit," called Pooh, rubbing his noisy belly. "What were you saying about breakfast?"

"I didn't say anything about breakfast," replied Rabbit, surprised. "Hmm," said Pooh thoughtfully. "Breakfast is such a wonderful notion, I was sure that you had mentioned it."

Rabbit sighed. "We can eat after I finish the weeding," he said. It's next on my list." Rabbit was proud of his list. He had rewritten, scratched out, erased, undone, and redone the list so many times that he knew by heart, without even checking, what came next.

And Pooh knew just what a Best Bear would do next. "Let me help, Rabbit," said Pooh. Then he began to pluck and pull, and pull and pluck until . . .

"Oh, no!" cried Rabbit. "You've picked all of my spinach!"

"I guess it'll be spinach toast for breakfast, spinach sandwiches for lunch, and spinach cakes for dinner from now on," grumped Rabbit.

"Oh, dear," said Pooh. He had only wanted to help his friend. Then a gentle rumble in his tummy made Pooh think that maybe he still could be of help. "Does honey go well with spinach toast?" he asked hopefully.

"Yes, yes, I'm sure that it does," said Rabbit, a little less crossly.

So with his tummy full and his mouth sticky from honey and spinach toast, Pooh left Rabbit with a much smaller pile of spinach to worry about, and set off to visit his friend Piglet.

Piglet lived in a lovely house snuggled inside a beech tree. He was almost finished with a thorough cleaning. He had wiped, washed, dusted, swept, picked up, and put away. All that was left to do was the mopping.

"Oh, hello, Pooh. I'm cleaning my house today," said Piglet.

Pooh was sure that a Best Bear would want to help a small friend with such a large job. "Let me help, Piglet," said Pooh.

Pooh began to mop. He soaped and splashed the floors. He soaped and splashed the furniture, the walls, and the ceiling. He made sure not to forget the closets, the pantry, and, of course, the windows.

Soon, soapy water was splashing everywhere—even bubbling on top of Piglet's little pink nose! "Thank you so very much, Pooh," said Piglet, pulling the mop from his friend. "I d-d-don't think I can stand any more help today."

"Are you sure, Piglet?" asked Pooh, who thought that there was a spot on Piglet's sofa that wasn't yet covered with bubbles.

"Very sure," said Piglet, who almost seemed to be pushing Pooh to the door. "Very, very, very sure." The door closed behind Pooh with a sudsy squish.

Pooh sighed and rubbed his head. Had he really been a good helper? A Best Bear in the World sort of helper?

Pooh walked through the field outside Piglet's house. With a flash of color, a butterfly fluttered nearby.

Pooh followed the butterfly through a valley of bright wildflow-ers until it landed directly on top of Eeyore's nose. "Hello, Eeyore," said Pooh. "I've been following your butterfly."

"Of course you are, Pooh. No one comes just to see me," he said gloomily.

"Yes, they do, Eeyore," said Pooh. Pooh wondered how a Best Bear would make Eeyore feel better. "Maybe you need a Cheering Up song. I shall make one up right now." Rolling on the soft grass, he began to sing:

"Oh, the Hundred-Acre Wood!
The honey is most especially good!
There are butterflies to catch and silly games to play.
There's a Tigger to put a bounce in your day.
And a Piglet's hand to hold as you chase
the heffalumps away.
And did I tell you?
The friendliest, best-iest, snap-crackle-iest donkey
named Eeyore lives there—hooray!"

Pooh looked at his friend. Eeyore's frown was as long as ever. "Oh, bother," said Pooh. "I guess my Cheering Up song didn't work."

"It cheered me right up," said Eeyore in his usual grumpy voice. "Some people get cheery just on the inside."

"Oh, dear," sighed Pooh. He didn't know what to think now. With little bounce left in his plump step, Pooh set off for his Thoughtful Spot.

Pooh wasn't at all sure that he really was a Best Bear after all. He was softly humming a Cheering Up song for himself when Christopher Robin arrived.

"Christopher Robin, do you think that a bear who was trying very hard to be a Best Bear would get his friends wet or gloomy or . . . spinachy?" asked Pooh.

"Silly old bear," said Christopher Robin, pulling the plump bear close for a hug. "A Best Bear always tries to help his friends. And you're *always* a Best Bear."

"I am?" said Pooh.

"Yes, you are — because you're always you," said Christopher Robin, "and I love you."